HARRY
THE HAPPY HOPPER

WRITTEN BY KRISTA DEMMEL   ILLUSTRATED BY NATHAN MAETZENER

Kaylu PUBLISHING

Published by Kaylu Publishing, Omaha, Nebraska.

Copyright © 2011 Krista Demmel

ISBN 978-0-9848516-0-7

Visit us on the web at www.kaylupublishing.com and www.harrythehappyhopper.com

Dedication

To my dad for always encouraging me to follow my dreams even when he didn't understand them. -Krista

To Hannah and Jeffrey for being by my side as I made this, literally. I love you! -Nathan

"Hurray, hurray, it's time to start another day!" said Harry the Happy Hopper as he hopped right out of bed.

Harry hopped to the window hoping to see a sunny morning, but instead he saw rain coming down from the dark gray clouds that filled the sky. Harry smiled and said, "I had hoped for a sunny day, but this rain is nice I must say! The flowers and trees will drink it up and grow, grow, grow." Harry loved the flowers and the trees.

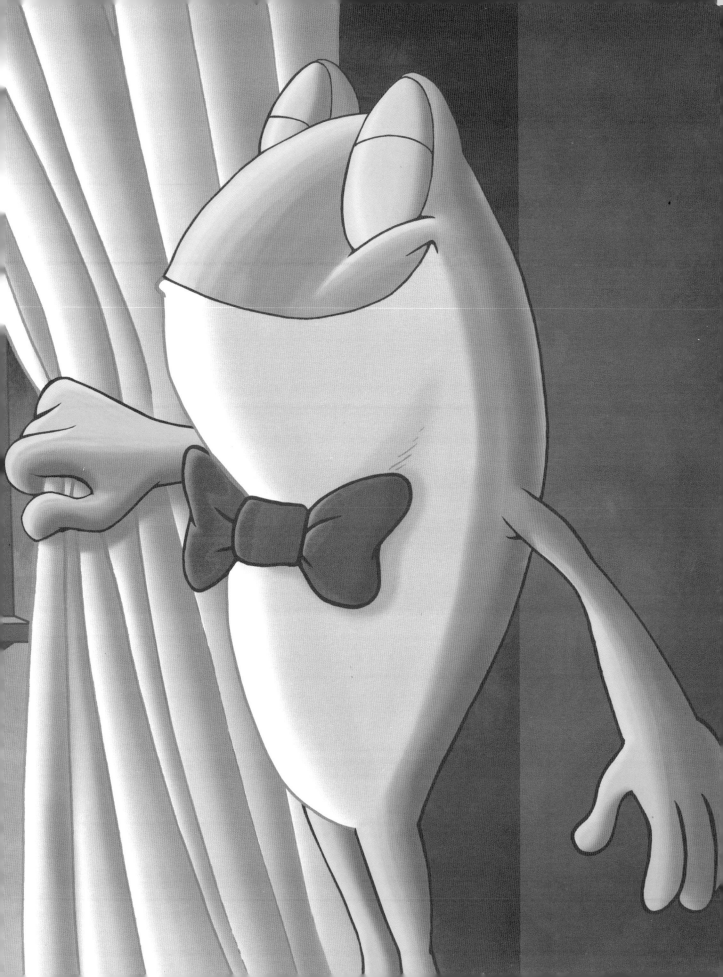

Harry got ready for the day remembering how much he enjoyed using his bright red umbrella. He was thankful to have such a beautiful umbrella to keep him dry.

Harry sang a happy song as he happily hopped along. "Pitter patter, pitter patter, drip, drip, drip... I'll wear my boots and skip, skip, skip."

And skip he did… Right past City Hall where the town's animals were having a meeting.

Mayor Mason the Mongoose saw Harry hop by and said to the quarreling town's animals, "If all of you were as happy as Harry the Happy Hopper I do believe we would have the happiest city on earth. Why do you think Harry is so happy?"

The town's animals had lots of ideas.
"Maybe he's rich and can buy whatever he wants!"
"Maybe everyone is nice to him!"
"Maybe he has a big, beautiful house!"

"I have an idea!" said Zayden the Zebra.
"We can follow Harry and see what in the world
makes Harry so happy and hoppy, and then,
we can be happy like Harry!"
"All right Zayden," said Mayor Mason. "You follow
him for a day to see how he always stays this way.
Then, come and tell us what you've found."

So Zayden the Zebra galloped out of the hall and down the street to catch up with Harry the Happy Hopper. He stayed back just a bit so Harry wouldn't see him.

"I bet Harry is happy because he has a lot of money to buy whatever he wants," Zayden thought to himself. He started to think about all the things Harry could buy that would make him happy... fun toys, his own swimming pool, and as much candy and ice cream as he could eat. "That's it!" Zayden thought. "I bet Harry is happy because he's rich!"

Just then Harry hopped into a store. Zayden was excited to see all the things Harry would buy. But to Zayden's surprise, Harry hopped right by the expensive toys and went to the grocery section. He only bought a few groceries, one candy bar and a bucket.
"Well," Zayden said, "Harry is not happy because he's rich. It must be because everyone is very nice to him."

As Harry stepped outside, he stopped and looked up at the sky. It had stopped raining, and now the sun was shining brightly. He breathed the fresh air deep into his lungs, and then he smiled as he began to hop along. "Something just made Harry happy," said Zayden, "but I didn't see what it was. I must watch more closely!"

Harry began to happily hop along, saying "hello" and
"good morning" to all the animals he met.
"*People* seem to make Harry very happy," said Zayden.
He wrote it down so he wouldn't forget.

But then, Zayden saw Old Ms. Melba the Mean Mule, the grumpiest lady in town, walking straight toward them. Zayden leaped behind a mailbox so he wouldn't be seen. He didn't want her to say anything mean to him.

However, Harry hopped right up to her and said,
"Good morning Ms. Melba! Isn't it a beautiful day?
I hope you're doing well!"
"Huh!" Melba the Mean Mule grunted.
"It certainly is NOT a beautiful day! It is quite dreadful
I do say! Must you say 'good morning' every day?!"

Zayden watched curiously as Harry kept smiling at her
even though she was so mean to him. Then, Zayden saw
something he could not understand. As Melba rushed by,
Harry slipped that candy bar right into her pocket. This
seemed to make Harry even happier, and he started to
whistle a happy song as he happily hopped along. Zayden
was confused, but he wrote everything down so he could
tell the town's animals.

Harry began to hop back to his house to cook lunch. Zayden followed close behind and thought about everything he had seen. "Well," Zayden said, "Harry isn't happy because he's rich, he isn't happy because everyone is nice to him, maybe he's happy because he has a big, beautiful house."

Harry turned down Hartman Street and hopped into a small, very ordinary house. Zayden was running out of ideas about Harry's happiness. "His house isn't big," Zayden said. "Maybe it's beautiful inside. I'll peek through the window."

Zayden sneaked up to a window and watched Harry
take his new bucket and place it under a leak in the roof.
Harry's house was not beautiful inside either. It was old
and plain, but Harry had a smile on his face as he began
to make lunch. He sang a happy song as he cooked.
"Chop, chop, chop. Hop, hop, hop. Throw it in the pan.
Plop, plop, plop."

As Zayden pondered Harry's happiness, the old box he stood on collapsed, and Zayden fell to the ground. "CRASH! BANG! THUD!"
Harry heard the crash and hopped out to see what was going on. "Zayden," Harry said, "Are you okay? What are you doing outside my window?"

"I'm okay," Zayden replied. "I'm just trying to figure out what makes you so happy and hoppy all the time, and I can't seem to figure it out. Tell me Harry, why are you so happy?"

Harry just smiled. He invited Zayden to come inside for lunch, and he began to teach him all about happiness.

Zayden and Harry shared a wonderful lunch, and Zayden learned a lot. He couldn't wait to get back to City Hall to tell the other animals.

As he trotted along, he sang a song just like Harry. "Tweet, tweet, tweet. Shuffle my feet. Being happy like Harry is sweet, sweet, sweet!"

When Zayden arrived he told the town's animals everything he had learned. "Sunshine makes Harry happy, but so does rain. Kind people make Harry happy, but so do grumpy people. Having a house makes Harry happy, even though it's small and old. The happiest people don't always have the best of everything; they just make the best of everything they have."

"Everyone has a choice," Zayden said.
"I suggest we choose to be happy just like Harry."
The town's animals agreed, and to this day,
Zayden and Harry live in the happiest city on earth.

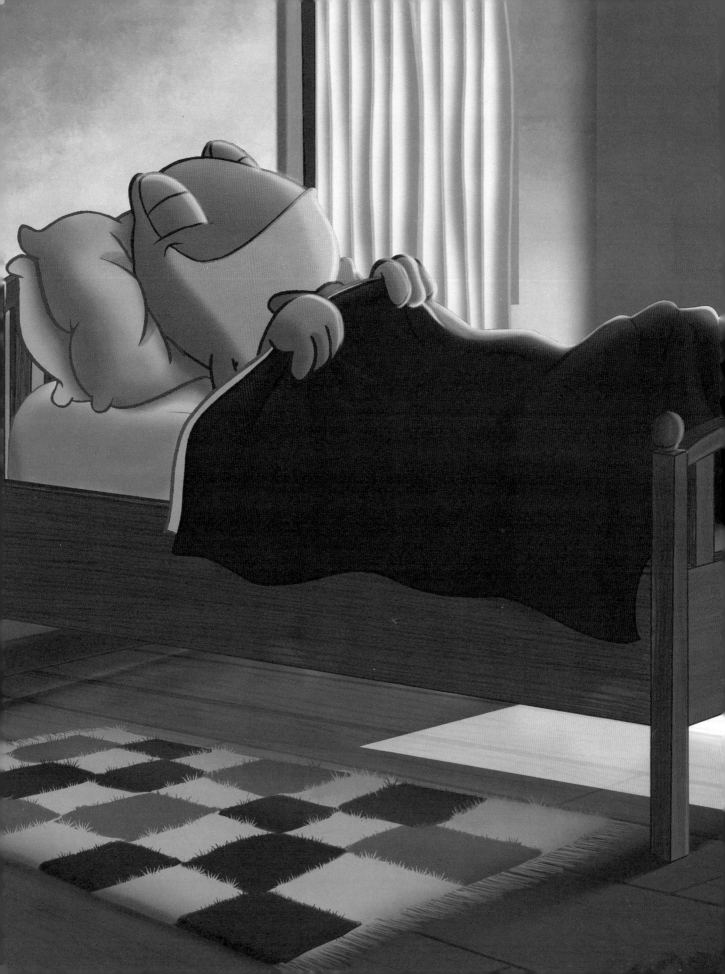

Harry the Happy Hopper went to bed that night happy for what he had even though it wasn't a lot. Harry was a happy hopper indeed, and he drifted off to sleep dreaming happy hoppy dreams.
Good night Harry!

Made in the USA
Charleston, SC
13 December 2011